For all moms
and substitute moms.

— RD + HZ

G. P. PUTNAM'S SONS,
a division of Penguin Putnam Books for Young Readers,
345 Hudson Street, New York, NY 10014.
G. P. Putnam's Sons, Reg. U.S. Pat. & Tm. Off. Published simultaneously in Canada.
Printed in China for Harriet Ziefert, Inc.
Jacket designed by Carolyn T. Fucile. Text set in Gill Sans.
The art was done in Flashe paint and ink on bristol board.
Library of Congress Cataloging-in-Publication Data
Ziefert, Harriet.   31 uses for a mom / Harriet Ziefert ;
drawings by Rebecca Doughty.   p.   cm.
Summary: Humorous drawings show some different ways in which moms serve their children.
[1. Mothers—Fiction.] I. Title: Thirty-one uses for a mom. II. Doughty, Rebecca, ill. III. Title.
PZ7.Z487 Aab 2003   [E]—dc21   2002007767
ISBN 0-399-23862-X
3 5 7 9 10 8 6 4 2
First Impression

31 USES for a MOM

Harriet Ziefert

drawings by Rebecca Doughty

G. P. Putnam's Sons   New York

1.
clock

2. chauffeur

3.
hairstylist

4. tailor

5. navigator

6.
doctor

7. pitcher

8. catcher

9. retriever

10. encyclopedia

11. accompanist

12. beach chair

13.
bottle opener

14. taster

15.
fixer-upper

16. photographer

17. tooth
puller

18. party planner

19.
ruler

20. opponent

21.
personal
shopper

22.
answering
service

23.
costume
designer

24. thermometer

25. pet sitter

26.
mixer

27. bank

28.
tweezer

29. hand holder

30.

page
turner

31.
friend